# TEENAGE MUTANT NINJA TURTLES™

# THE OFFICIAL NINJA TURTLE HANDBOOK

## RANDOM HOUSE 🏠 NEW YORK

© 2014 Viacom International Inc. and Viacom Overseas Holdings C.V. All rights reserved. Published in the United States by Random House Children's Books, a division of Random House LLC, 1745 Broadway, New York, NY 10019, and in Canada by Random House of Canada Limited, Toronto, Penguin Random House Companies. Random House and the colophon are registered trademarks of Random House LLC. Nickelodeon, Teenage Mutant Ninja Turtles, and all related titles, logos, and characters are trademarks of Viacom International Inc. and Viacom Overseas Holdings C.V. Based on characters created by Peter Laird and Kevin Eastman.

randomhouse.com/kids

ISBN 978-0-553-50768-3

Printed in the United States of America
10 9 8 7 6 5 4 3

# CONTENTS

# SPLINTER

The mutated rat known as Splinter once had a human life. As Hamato Yoshi, he was the leader of a great ninja clan in Japan. That was before his rival, Oroku Saki, killed his wife and daughter and forced him to flee to America. There, Yoshi was doused with mutagen that transformed him into a giant rat. His four pet turtles were also mutated. Splinter raised the turtles as his sons, eventually training them to become ninja masters.

# LEONARDO

Leonardo is the leader of the Ninja Turtles. He desperately wants to be the best ninja in the group and takes every opportunity to flaunt his skills. Leonardo knows this can make him seem like a show-off, but he hopes his example will inspire his brothers. His favorite show, *Space Heroes*, often teaches him valuable leadership lessons.

# RAPHAEL

**T**he biggest and toughest Turtle, Raphael is a straight-up brawler who has very little patience for things like stealth, hiding in shadows, and keeping his voice down. He would rather hit first and ask questions later. Though he's fiercely loyal to his brothers, he enjoys giving them a hard time. His closest confidant is his pet turtle, Spike, whom he rescued from the sewer.

# DONATELLO

Donatello is the team's brilliant inventor. He can make amazing gadgets, weapons, and vehicles with items scavenged from the trash. Donatello likes order and logic, and is often impatient that his brothers can't keep up with him intellectually. This all makes Donnie the most socially awkward of the Turtles—especially when his not-very-secret crush, April, is nearby.

# MICHELANGELO

The youngest and most energetic of the Turtles, Michelangelo is also the most lighthearted and easily distracted. This happy lack of focus gives his martial arts a "flow" the other Turtles cannot match. When he's not battling, Mikey loves a good practical joke. His brothers always have to be on the lookout for a water balloon from "Dr. Prankenstein."

# THE LAIR

**D**eep beneath the streets of New York City, in an abandoned subway station, is the Turtles' lair. This is their home and secret headquarters. Here they train, make plans, and build inventions. Each Turtle has his own room, but there is also a common room, where they watch TV, skateboard, play video games, and eat pizza.

Most importantly, the lair contains the Turtles' *dojo,* the combined gym and classroom where Splinter teaches his ninja sons martial arts skills and Zen philosophy.

# NINJUTSU

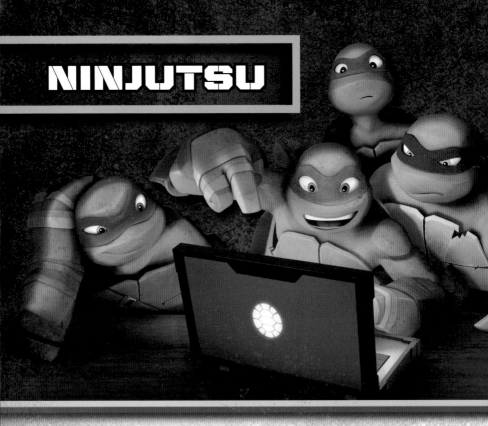

**N**injas use their minds as well as their might. They outwit their enemies and use their environment to their advantage.

A ninja makes no unnecessary movements and wastes no words. A true ninja does not receive accolades because he or she is a stealthy creature of the night. It is a hard existence that requires absolute devotion to the martial arts.

Ninjas know that a good plan has as few steps as possible. A ninja strikes but once.

# NINJUTSU GLOSSARY

**kunoichi** — a female ninja.

**ninjutsu** — properly translated, ninjutsu means "the art of endurance." It is the martial art of the ninja.

**ninniku seishin** — the ability to endure insults with patience. A ninja never loses his or her cool.

**seiza** — the traditional kneeling position, used both for resting between training sessions and as a way to meditate.

**sensei** — a teacher, both of discipline and philosophy.

**shinobi shozuku** — the ninja's traditional black outfit.

**soryu** — a fighting style passed from teacher to student.

**tanto** — a short multipurpose knife.

**L**eonardo is skilled with his *katana*, which are sharp and finely crafted from steel. He can wield two at the same time as if they are one blade.

# KATANA

Raphael is armed with a weapon called a *sai*. It consists of a long blade flanked by two short, sharp prongs. Raphael can use his *sai* to block an enemy's attack or to make a point of his own.

# SAI

**T**hough Donatello can make any weapon he wants, nothing compares to his *bo* staff. This is a long staff with a blade at the end.

# BO STAFF

Michelangelo's weapons of choice are *nunchucks*. Made of two hard sticks connected by a chain, *nunchucks* can be spun to deliver a striking blow, or they can be used defensively.

# NUNCHUCKS

# SHELLRAISER

Built with scavenged parts and an old subway car, this armored assault vehicle is the Turtles' ultimate weapon. It can travel on city streets and subway tracks. Its weapons include steamrollers and claws for tearing down barriers, and a trash cannon and manhole-cover launcher. Inside the van, Leonardo drives, Raphael handles the weapons, Michelangelo navigates, and Donatello is the chief engineer.

SHELLRAISER

# STEALTH BIKE

**H**idden inside the *Shellraiser*, Raphael's three-wheeled chopper deploys a shell-shaped shield that allows it to blend perfectly with the pavement. Its electric motor runs silently to avoid detection.

# PATROL BUGGY

**T**his four-man dune buggy splits into four separate go-karts, one for each of the Turtles. Its low profile and sharp handling make it ideal for maneuvering through narrow alleys and crowded city streets.

# APRIL O'NEIL

**A**pril thought she was a regular sixteen-year-old girl, until extradimensional invaders captured her father, Kirby O'Neil, a world-famous scientist. Now she's on a mission to find her dad, her best friends are the mutant Turtles, and she's discovering that she has psychic powers that make her necessary to the alien invasion. To help her through all this, Splinter is teaching her to become a *kunoichi*.

# CASEY JONES

**T**his teenage vigilante is a good friend of the Turtles. He loves to play hockey and he loves fighting crime. He's a skilled but untrained martial artist who can be hotheaded and arrogant.

# ICE CREAM KITTY

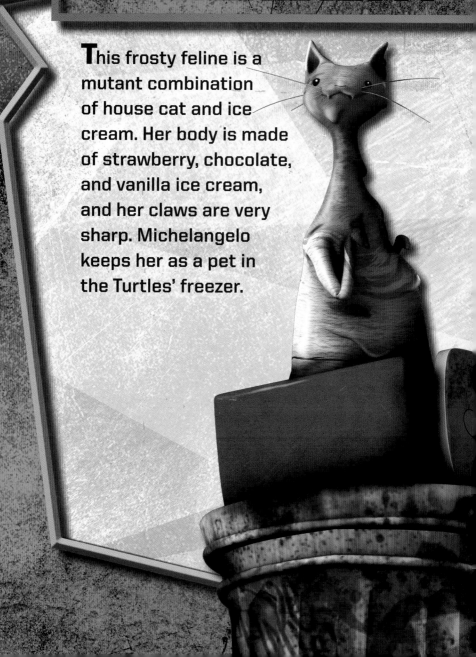

This frosty feline is a mutant combination of house cat and ice cream. Her body is made of strawberry, chocolate, and vanilla ice cream, and her claws are very sharp. Michelangelo keeps her as a pet in the Turtles' freezer.

# KRAANG

The Kraang are brainlike invaders from another dimension. Because their home is becoming uninhabitable, they are trying to transform Earth's environment into one suitable for them. Their headquarters are in the offices of the mysterious company TCRI, which stands for Techno Cosmic Research Institute.

# MUTAGEN

The Kraang's main weapon is a powerful chemical mutagen sometimes called ooze. A little drop can mutate anything it touches. It can make normal creatures bigger and stronger, and it can combine the DNA of different species to make completely new beings.

# KRAANG-DROID

**T**he Kraang occupy android "hosts" called Kraang-droid that enable them to perform day-to-day activities. They can walk, talk, fight, and even eat.

# SHREDDER

This evil underworld boss was known as Oroku Saki when he lived in Japan. It was there that he destroyed Splinter's wife and daughter. Now, living in New York City, Shredder leads the Foot Clan. Hidden behind an armor of blades, he works to destroy Splinter and the Ninja Turtles.

# KARAI

Karai is a cunning and strong-willed *kunoichi*. She is fiercely loyal to her teacher and father, Shredder. She even leads the Foot Clan in his absence. She long believed that Splinter had killed her mother. It was later revealed that Karai is Miwe, Splinter's long-lost daughter.

# FOOTBOTS

The Kraang created these robotic warriors and gave them to Shredder to help him destroy the Turtles. With a rotating saw and a giant blade for hands, they are dangerous and deadly. They are programmed to mimic and instantly counter an opponent's moves.

# THE FOOT CLAN

**S**hredder leads a vast army of ninja warriors known as the Foot Clan. Originally from Japan, they are fearless and obey him without question. They wear identical black uniforms when in action. The Foot Clan come from all walks of life and often plot and fight in their civilian identities as well.

# FOOT CLAN BIKE

**T**he Foot Clan's favorite way to get around, these slick black bikes sport a dragon head, defensive spikes, and a flag with the Foot Clan emblem. They're fast and nimble—perfect for high-speed pursuits of the Turtles.

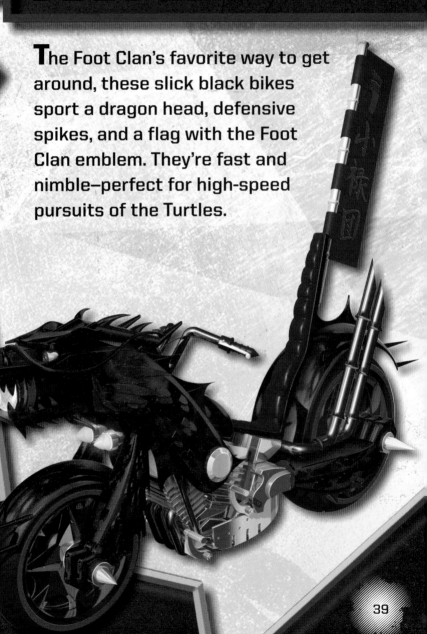

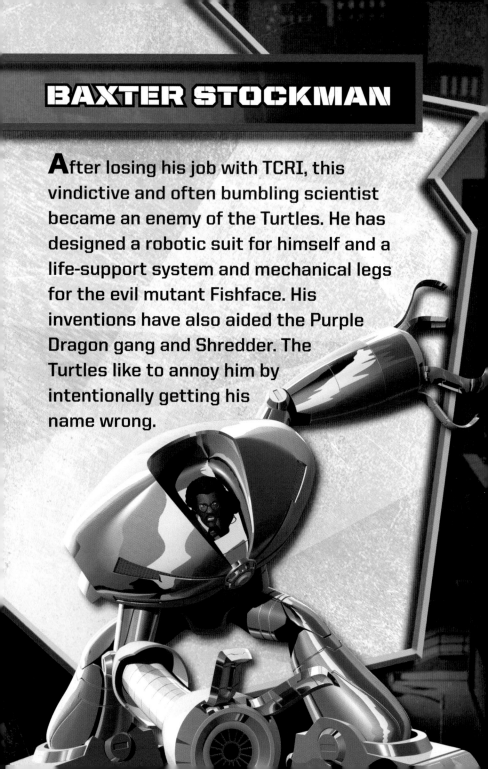

# BAXTER STOCKMAN

**A**fter losing his job with TCRI, this vindictive and often bumbling scientist became an enemy of the Turtles. He has designed a robotic suit for himself and a life-support system and mechanical legs for the evil mutant Fishface. His inventions have also aided the Purple Dragon gang and Shredder. The Turtles like to annoy him by intentionally getting his name wrong.

# MOUSERS

**T**hese Mobile Offensive Underground Search Excavation and Retrieval Sentries are small robots designed by Baxter Stockman. Their size makes them ideal for finding hidden passageways in and out of banks, power stations, and other secure areas. They are controlled with a pheromone spray.

# DOGPOUND

**C**hris Bradford was an arrogant martial arts star and a student of the evil ninja master Shredder. But a dog bite and a splash of mutagen changed him into Dogpound. He's now a powerful enemy of the Turtles and remains fiercely loyal to Shredder.

# RAHZAR

**D**uring a battle with Mikey at TCRI, Dogpound fell into a giant vat of mutagen. The result was a bigger, stronger, more mutated monster called Rahzar. He has long fangs, massive metallic claws and spikes, and a protective exoskeleton.

# SNAKEWEED

Snake was a common thug until he was splashed with some mutagen during a fight with the Turtles. His DNA combined with that of a plant and he grew to nearly thirty feet!
The Turtles destroyed him once by freezing him, but weeds have a habit of popping up again and again. . . .

# MAD MONKEY

**D**r. Tyler Rockwell was a brilliant scientist who was changed into a giant monkey by his devious partner, Dr. Falco. He retained much of his intelligence and developed telepathic powers.

# FISHFACE

**X**ever was a low-level thug until Shredder plucked him out of prison to do his bidding. After being exposed to a mutagen bomb, he became Fishface, a mutant with a poisonous bite. Baxter Stockman built him robot legs and a breathing device so he can continue to track down and battle the Turtles.

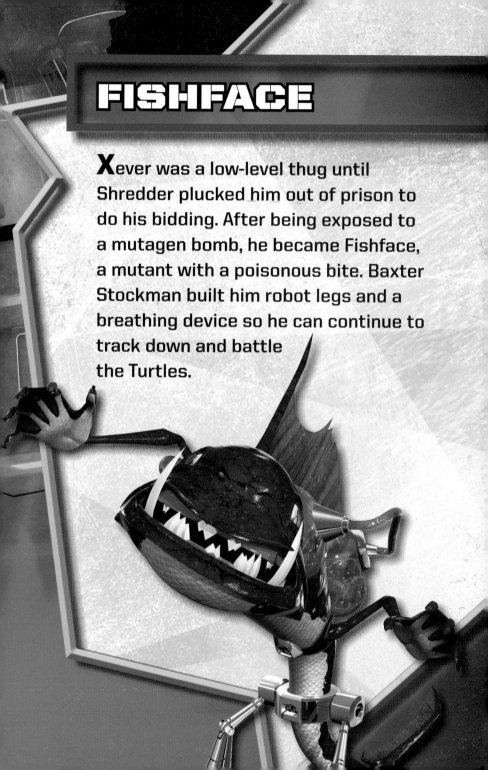

# THE RAT KING

**D**r. Victor Falco was a talented but ruthless scientist who teamed up with the Kraang. He used their mutagen to create a serum that enabled psychic powers. He tested it on himself and became a giant human/rat hybrid who can telepathically control rats. No rat mind—not even Splinter's—is safe from his powers.

# LEATHERHEAD

This powerful reptilian mutant started life as a normal pet alligator, but he was flushed down the toilet and captured by the Kraang. Before he could escape, they experimented on him, making him large, strong, and very angry.

His martial arts skills aren't as developed as the Turtles', but his incredible strength—and rage—makes him a powerful, if unpredictable, ally in the Turtles' fight against the Kraang. He really likes Michelangelo's Pizza Noodle Soup.

# PIGEON PETE

**W**hile developing mutagen, the Kraang experimented on dozens of animals and humans. Pete is the result of one of these experiments. His combined pigeon and human DNA allows him to fly and speak. Though he's excitable and has a short attention span, he can be helpful to the Turtles.

# NEWTRALIZER

**A**ccidentally released from a Kraang prison by Donnie, the Newtralizer is a large reptilian creature loaded with weapons, including lasers, missiles, saw blades, and mines. Though he's an enemy of the Kraang, he doesn't like the Turtles much either.

# SQUIRRELANOIDS

These are not your average cute and fuzzy squirrels. Mutagen has made them big, strong, and vicious. They multiply in people's stomachs, grow quickly, and *love* popcorn. Mikey's knowledge of comic-book monsters comes in handy when the Turtles are fighting these nutty nightmares.

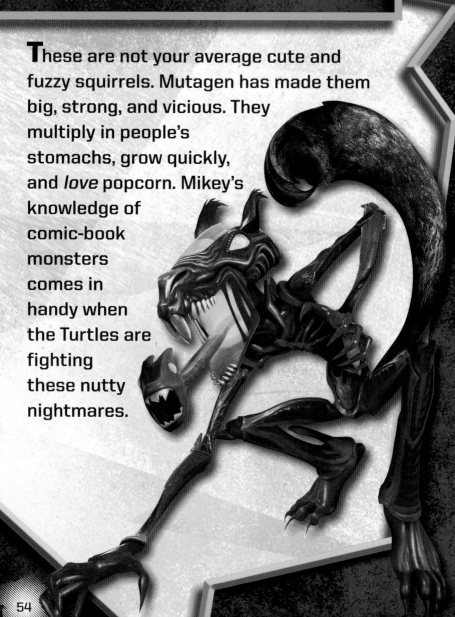

# PARASITICA

**A**nother Kraang mutagen experiment gone bad, this enormous parasitic wasp has the power to brainwash its victims with a simple sting.

# COCKROACH TERMINATOR

**W**hen Donnie outfitted a common cockroach with surveillance gear to spy on the Kraang, it seemed like a great idea—until the bug fell into a vat of mutagen. Now the bug is a giant mechanized monster who's gone rogue. This really bothers Raph because he has a fear of cockroaches.

# SPIDER-BYTEZ

**T**his spider/human hybrid was originally a rude New Yorker named Vic. He didn't like the Turtles, or as he called them, the "Kung-Fu Frogs." During a fight with the Kraang, some mutagen splattered on him. He transformed into Spider-Bytez, a mean-spirited mutant with increased strength who can spit acid and shoot super-strong webs.

# KIRBY BAT

**T**his mutation is personal for the Turtles. Their friend April O'Neil was in danger of being hit with mutagen, but her father, Kirby, pushed her out of the way—and got splashed himself. He became Kirby Bat, a giant red-bearded, middle-aged bat.

# TIGER CLAW

**T**his bounty hunter from Japan is a tiger/human hybrid. He began life as a circus performer, but after being mutated, he became one of Shredder's most dreaded henchmen. Tiger Claw lost his tail in a battle and has been hunting the soldier who took it ever since.

# SLASH

**W**hen mutagen is accidentally spilled in Raphael's room, his pet turtle, Spike, is splashed. The result is a massive, super-violent ninja turtle. At first, Raphael thinks he can team up with his old friend. However, he quickly realizes that the giant turtle is too mean and strong to be controlled. Spike goes rogue and becomes . . . Slash.

# MUTAGEN MAN

**W**hen Tim, a mild-mannered ice cream vendor, first saw the Turtles in action, he knew he wanted to be a crime fighter. So he made himself a costume and became the Pulverizer. During a battle with Dogpound, he doused himself with mutagen, hoping to gain super strength. Instead, he became Mutagen Man, a strange blob with an acidic touch.